END

START

**Robot HD29 is turning 5 years old today.
Can you help him find the way to his birthday cake?**

1

START

END

LawnBot has just finished trimming a hedge maze.
Can you help him find the way out?

END

START

Uh-oh—Robot CD2 has let go of her balloon!
Luckily she can walk up walls.
Can you help her
find her way to the balloon?

SubBot is searching for a sunken treasure. Can you help him find his way to the fortune at the bottom of the ocean?

START

END

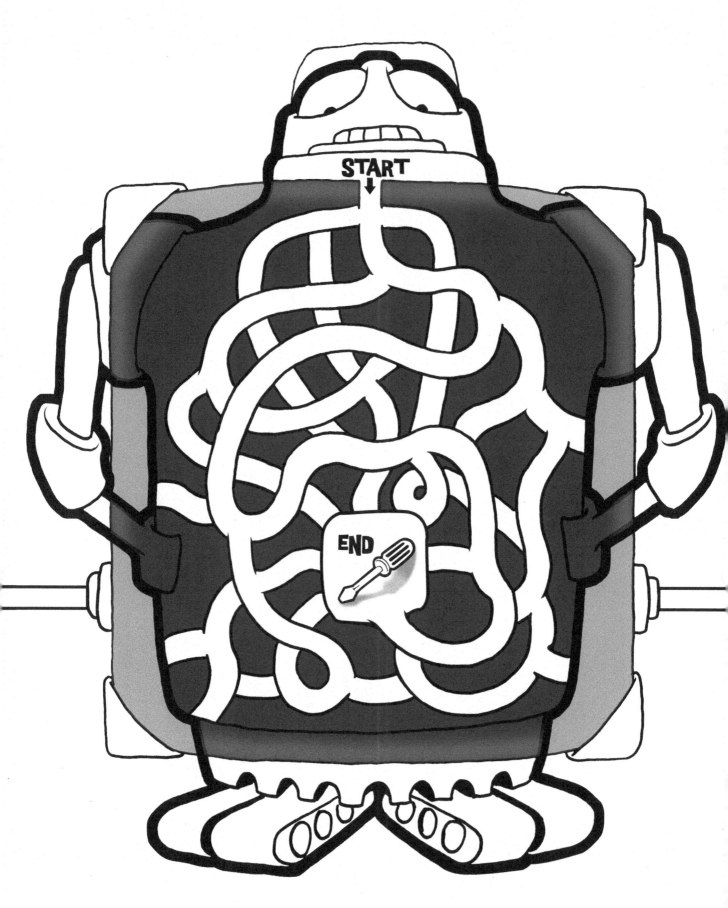

START

END

Robot PD6 has accidentally swallowed a screwdriver!
Can you help get it out?

MoonBot has collected some rocks on the moon.
Can you help her find the way
back to the spaceship?

START

END

7

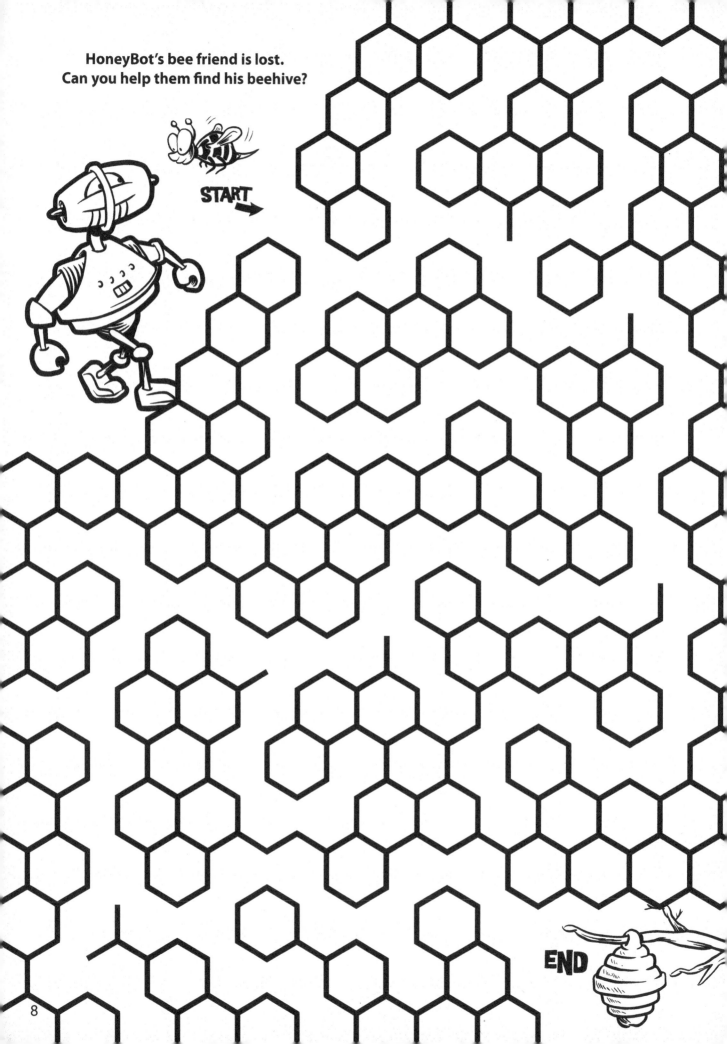

HoneyBot's bee friend is lost.
Can you help them find his beehive?

START

END

There's a big traffic jam on the highway.
Can you help Robot BD12 find her way through it?

END

START

END

START

The BaseBots have lost their ball
on top of the maze.
Can you help them get it back?

END

START

TileBot is laying down a kitchen floor, but he needs to fix some corners...

...can you get him through the white tiles to his toolbox?

START

Robot MD1 was flying
home when he came upon
a hot-air balloon festival.
Can you help him make his way
through the balloons and clouds?

A **B** **C**

Robot: _____ **Robot:** _____ **Robot:** _____

These robots have gotten their long necks mixed up together.
Can you match the robots to their heads?

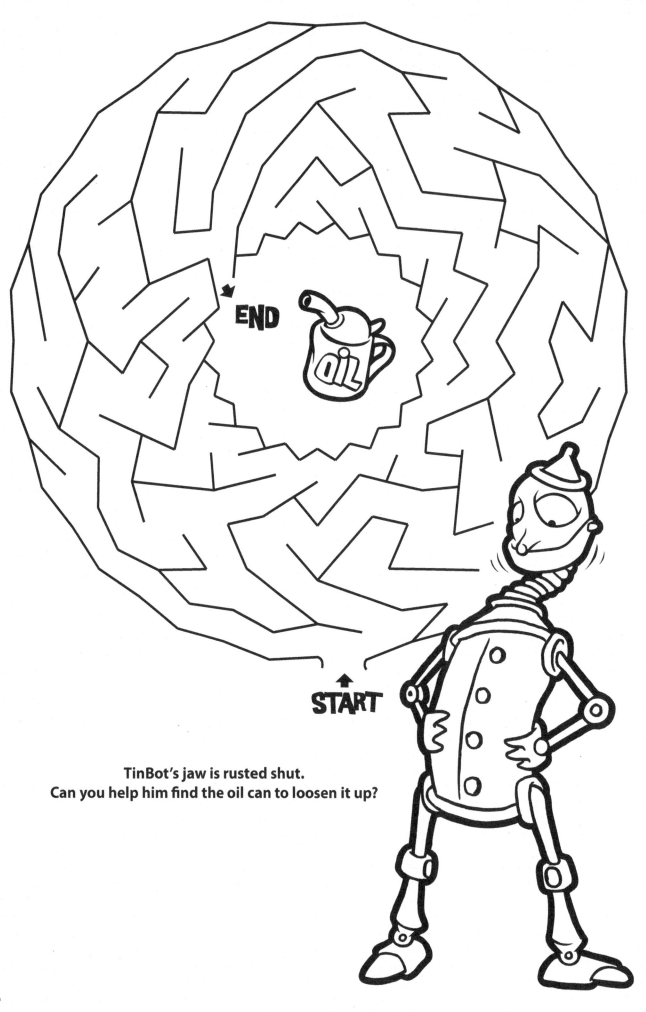

END

OIL

START

TinBot's jaw is rusted shut.
Can you help him find the oil can to loosen it up?

END

1ST

START

Robot LB10 has won a sand-castle competition!
Can you help her claim her 1st-place ribbon?

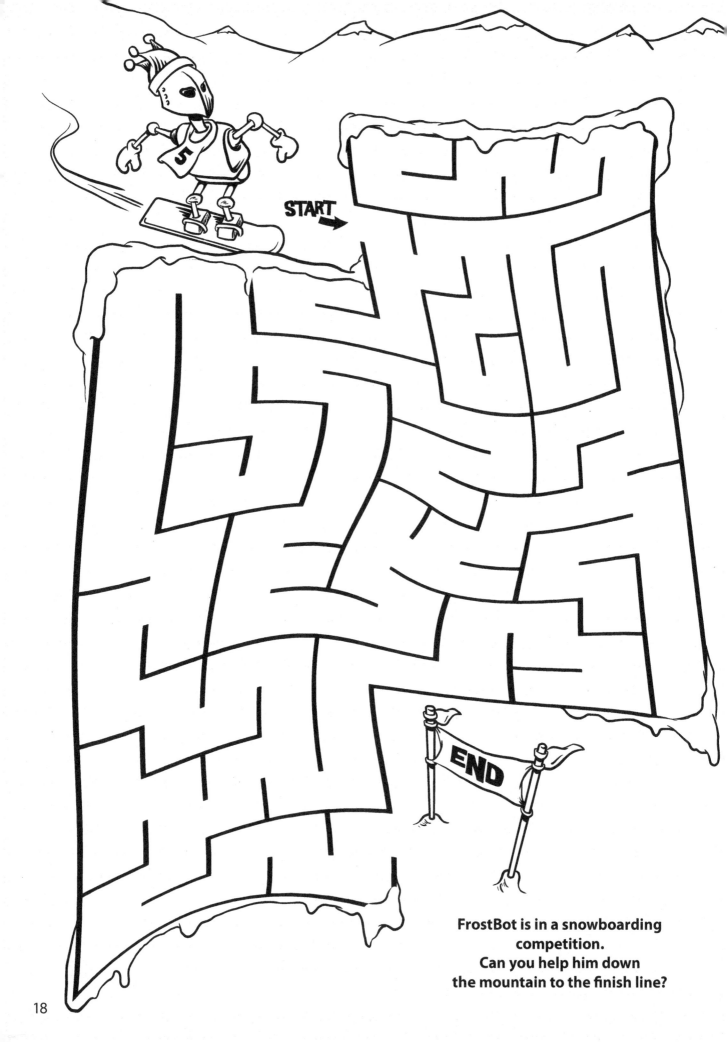

START →

END

FrostBot is in a snowboarding
competition.
Can you help him down
the mountain to the finish line?

END

START

It's Halloween, and TrikBot and TreatBot
are headed for the castle.
Can you help them find the way?
(Be careful! You might have to go through some tunnels.)

19

Robot K9 is a dog walker.
Can you help her and her puppy buddies
find their way to the dog park?

START

END

END

Uh-oh!
The lighthouse light is out!
Can you help Robot LH find
his way to the top to fix it?

START

START

Robot KD8 was flying in space
when he came across a meteor shower!
Can you help him through the rocks and
comets to safety?

END

END

RockBot is a mountain climber who
needs help getting up this mountain.
Can you help him reach the top?

START

24

END

Robot WD70 was out for a walk when she came upon a swamp. Can you help her get across to the dock?

START

25

The fire alarm has gone off!
Can you find out which hose is
connected to the fire hydrant?

A   B   C   D

26

END

START

There's no fire after all—
a kitten is stuck in a tree!
Can you help the firefighters rescue her?

FIR

START

The robot track team is practicing for the relay race.
Can you help them pass the baton to each other
all the way to the finish line?

END

DigBot 2000 is searching for a treasure. Can you help her find the right tunnel to the buried chest?

START

END

MasonBot is laying down bricks for a new apartment building. Can you help him find his way to the top of the wall?

END

START

31

START

END

Can you help Robot JS27's legs
find the way to reach his top half?

Can you help PlumbBot clear the clogged sink?

(You might have to go behind some pipes to get there!)

START

END

START

END

TeleBot has fixed the satellite dish on the rooftop. Can you help him find the way back inside the building?

34

END

START

**TraxBot is missing one of his tracks!
Can you help him find it?**

START

Can you go around
EndBot to find
your way to the end?

END

36

Solutions

PG. 1

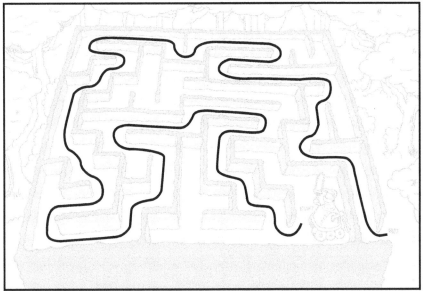

PGS. 2 and **3**

PG. 4

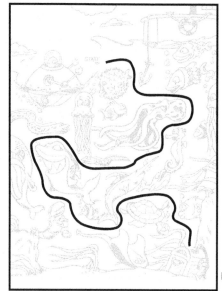

PG. 5

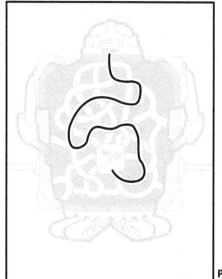

PG. 6

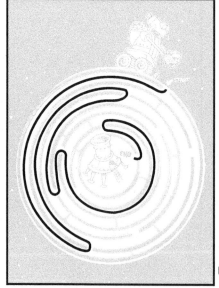

PG. 7

38

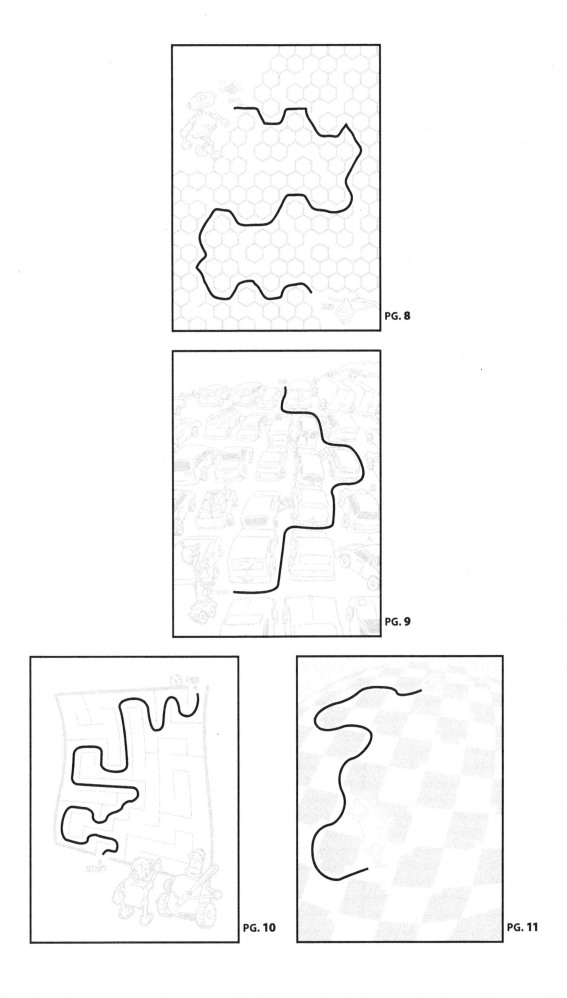

PG. 8

PG. 9

PG. 10

PG. 11

PGS. 12 and **13**

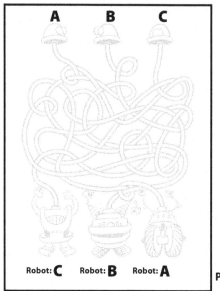

A   B   C

Robot: **C**   Robot: **B**   Robot: **A**   **PG. 14**

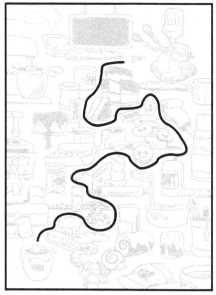

PG. 15

PG. 16

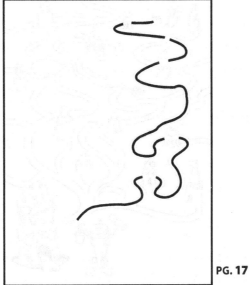

PG. 17

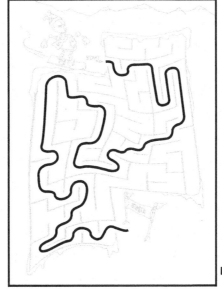

PG. 18

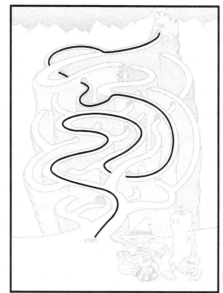

PG. 19

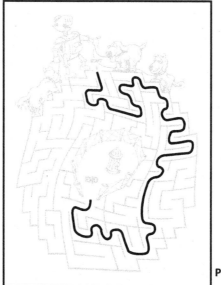

PG. 20

PG. 21

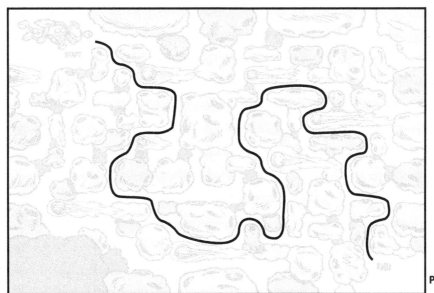

PGS. 22 and **23**

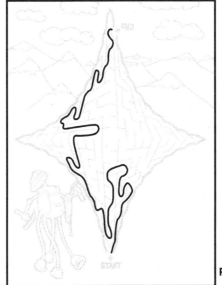

PG. 24

PG. 25

PG. 26

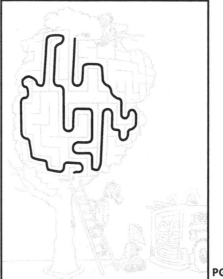

PG. 27

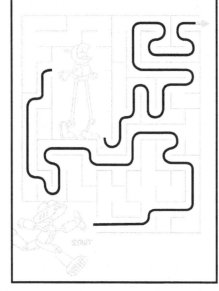

PG. 28

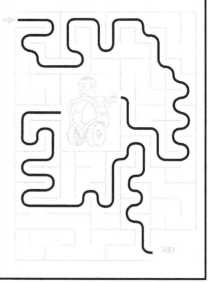

PG. 29

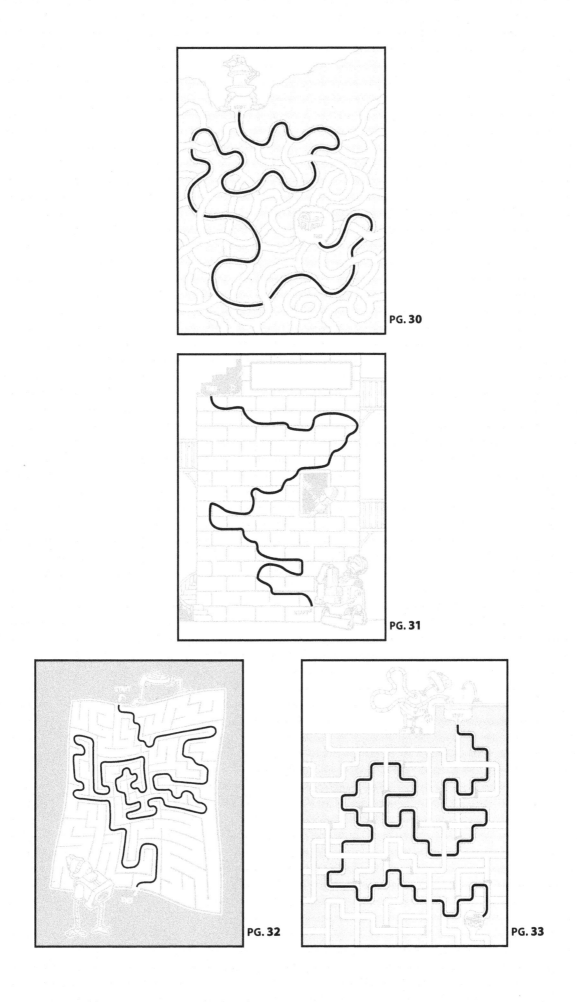

PG. 30

PG. 31

PG. 32

PG. 33

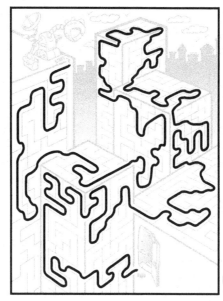

PG. **34**

PG. **35**

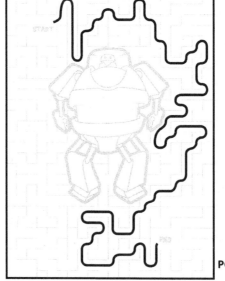

PG. **36**